Night Night, GROOT

Written by Brendan Deneen
Artwork by Cale Atkinson

PaRRagon

Bath · New York · Cologne · Melbourne · Delhi
Hong Kong · Shenzhen · Singapore

Night Night, GROOT,

it's time for bed.
Time to rest
your sleepy head.

The day was long and filled with fun.
Think of all the things you've done!

You played games with friends ...

and you jumped around.

Now it's time to settle down.

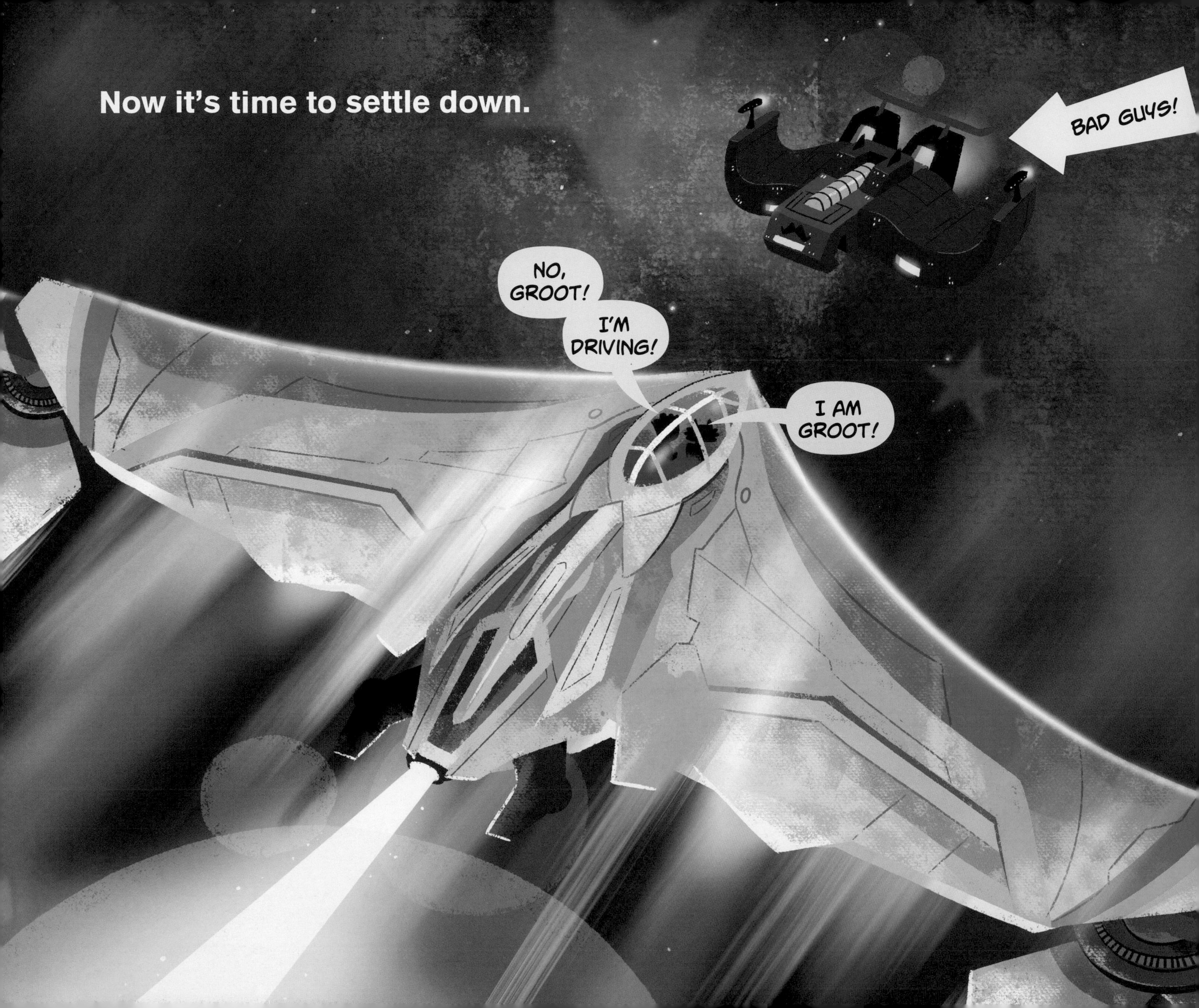

Night night, tiny little tree.
Time to let your dreams run free.

And do not fear on your dreamland ride ...

even the Hulks
are on your side!

FOCUS, GROOT!

Your friends will keep bad dreams away.

Your friends are here
to save the day.

They'll bring their kicks
and a spin attack!

They'll keep watch over you and guard the door.

They'll lift those bad guys off the floor.

**Wonderful things happened so fast,
Making the day quite a blast!**

The day is now done and super friends say:

'Night night, Groot.
You've had a wonderful day.'

The End